The Surprise

Günter Gerngross

HELBLING LANGUAGES
www.helblinglanguages.com

The Surprise
by Günter Gerngross
© HELBLING LANGUAGES 2007

All rights reserved. No part of this publication may be reproduced, stored in a retrieval system, or transmitted, in any form or by any means, electronic, mechanical, photocopying, recording, or otherwise, without the prior written permission of the publishers.

First published 2007

ISBN 978-3-85272-004-3

The publishers would like to thank the following for their kind permission to reproduce the following photographs and othe copyright material: Alamy p30.

Series editor Maria Cleary
Illustrated by Marzia Sanfilippo
Activities by Elspeth Rawstron
Design and layout by Capolinea
Printed by Athesia

About this Book

For the Student

Listen to all of the story and do some activities on your Audio CD

Talk about the story

pets● When you see the green dot you can check the word in the glossary

For the Teacher

Go to our Readers Resource site for information on using readers and downloadable Resource Sheets, photocopiable Worksheets, Answer Keys and Tapescripts.

Plus the full version of the story on MP3.
www.helblinglanguages.com/readers

For lots of great ideas on using Graded Readers consult Reading Matters, the Teacher's Guide to using Helbling Readers.

Level 2 Structures

Past simple of *be*	Comparative
Past simple	Comparative with *as...as*
Past simple (common irregular verbs)	Superlative
Be going to	*To* for purpose
Past Continuous	Adverbs of manner
Past simple v. past continuous	
	A lot of, not much, not many
Past simple in questions	*And, so, but, because*
Have to / *Must*	Possessive pronouns
Mustn't	

Structures from lower levels are also included

3

Contents

Before Reading 6
The Surprise 9
After Reading 26

Before Reading

Meet Dacty

Hello, I'm the hero of the story. My name's Dacty and I'm a pterodactyl.
Pterodactyls were flying reptiles.
They had large wings and they flew long distances. Some had wings of over 12 metres in length. They lived in the Jurassic period, 150 million years ago. They died out 65 million years ago. They were carnivores and they ate meat and fish.

1 Answer the questions.

   a) What were pterodactyls?
   b) When did they live?
   c) When did they die out?
   d) What did they eat?

2 In pairs, look quickly at the pictures in the book. Discuss and answer the questions.

   a) The story is called 'The Surprise'. What do you think the surprise is?
   b) Why is Dacty a hero? What do you think he does?

Before Reading

3 Match the characters from the story with the descriptions.

a) b) c) d)

1 ☐ Hello, I'm Aunt Elizabeth. I've got curly red hair and I wear glasses. I work in a museum and I like travelling. Some people think that I'm strange. What do you think?

2 ☐ Hello. My name's Eric. I've got short grey hair and I'm wearing a mask. People don't like me. Can you guess why? Yes, I'm a thief.

3 ☐ Hi! My name's Roger. I've got short blond hair. When I'm not at school, I usually wear jeans. I've got a sister called Helen and a very unusual pet.

4 ☐ Hello, I'm Mrs Phillips. I've got long dark brown hair. Today, I'm wearing a green necklace and green earrings. I live with my husband, my two children and a flying reptile called Dacty!

4 Write a short description of this character in the story.

5 Who do you think he is?

7

The Surprise

It's Saturday evening. Mr and Mrs Phillips and their children, Roger and Helen, are playing cards in the living room. Suddenly• the telephone rings in the hall. Mr Phillips gets up and answers it. When he comes back he is smiling.

"That was your Aunt Elizabeth. She's back• from Greenland. She's coming to see us tomorrow morning. And she's got a surprise• for you two."

"A surprise for us! What is it?" Roger and Helen shout.
"I don't know," says their dad. "She says that it's a secret. And now it's time for bed."
"Come on, dad, one more game."
"Oh, okay. Then straight to bed!"

- **she's back:** she is home
- **suddenly:** that happens quickly when you don't expect it
- **surprise:** something you are not expecting

9

The next morning the doorbell rings. Roger and Helen run to open the door. It's Aunt Elizabeth, and she's got a big metal box. She hugs• the children. Then she opens the box very carefully. It's full of small pieces of ice. She puts her hand into the ice and she slowly takes out a big egg. "This egg is from an ice cave in Greenland. It's very special. Now I need your help."

"What do you want us to do?" ask the children.

"I want to see what happens when we put the egg in a warm place. There is no heating in my office at the museum• during the summer," says Aunt Elizabeth. "I thought I could leave it here."

"Yippee! An experiment!" shout the children.

They get a cardboard box and put the egg inside. Then they put the box next to the radiator• in the kitchen.

Glossary

- **hugs:** puts her arms around in a friendly way
- **museum:** place with lots of very old and precious objects
- **radiator:** heater, usually fixed to a wall (see page 11)

10

The Surprise

Aunt Elizabeth comes to check the egg every day but nothing happens. Then, one day while the children are having their breakfast they hear a noise.
"Look at the egg," shouts Helen. "Something's happening. It's cracking•."
Slowly a long beak• appears. "It's a bird," says Roger.
"No, it isn't," answers Helen. "It hasn't got any feathers."
"Of course it's a bird, stupid. Baby birds haven't got feathers."
The animal opens its beak.
"Let's give it a sausage," says Roger.
Helen gives a sausage to the animal. The animal is very hungry. It eats five sausages, two cooked tomatoes and six pieces of toast•.

- **beak:** hard pointed part of a bird's mouth
- **cracking:** breaking
- **toast:** grilled bread

A month later the family are having dinner.
"That thing's growing very fast," says mum.
"And it's always very hungry," answers Helen. "Roger thinks that it's a bird, but I don't think so. It still hasn't got any feathers."
"What does Aunt Elizabeth say?" asks mum.
"I don't know, she's away on another trip• and she isn't coming back for a few weeks."
"Let's check what it is," dad says and gets up.

At that moment the animal spreads• its wings, flies over to the table and grabs• dad's fish. The children laugh. Mum is not so happy.
"Get off the table," she shouts.
Dad goes to his computer.
"Hey, come and look! I know what it is! It's a pterodactyl."
"A pterodactyl?" shout the children.
"Yes, they lived a long, long time ago. They're a type of dinosaur. Pterodactyls can fly." "Yes, we know that, dad." say the children and laugh.
Dad sits down at the table. "Where's my fish?" he asks.
"Look at Dacty, dad. He's got it" Helen says.
"Now he's got a name," says mum. "Dacty sounds nice. It suits him•."

Glossary

- **grabs:** takes quickly
- **it suits him:** it is right for him
- **spreads:** opens wide
- **trip:** short journey

The Surprise

A few days later the children are in Helen's room.
"What are you doing with the bandage•?" asks Roger.
"There is something wrong with Dacty's wing. My room is too small and he keeps• banging• his wings against the walls and furniture. He can't fly. I feel sorry for him. And he is always hungry. Can you get something for him from the kitchen?"
Roger goes into the kitchen and cooks a big plate of sausages.
Helen helps Dacty down from her wardrobe. Roger puts the plate with the sausages in front of Dacty and the pterodactyl quickly eats them all up. Then he tries to fly on to the top of Helen's wardrobe, but he can't.

Mum, we have to take Dacty to a vet•. He can't fly. There's something wrong with his wing. Can you take us?"
"All right. Put him into the big basket."
"And mum, don't tell the vet that he is a pterodactyl," says Helen. "We don't want people to find out we've got a dinosaur in our house. There'll be stories in all the newspapers."
"Okay, I won't say a word," says mum.

When they get to the surgery• the vet looks very carefully at Dacty.
"The wing is not broken, but it needs rest. I'll put a splint• on it and it will be better soon. But what sort of bird is this? What happened to his feathers?"
"Oh, he's a special turkey• from South America, and they don't have feathers," says Roger. "Oh, yes, of course," says the vet. But she looks a little confused.

Glossary

- **bandage:** a long piece of cloth you tie around a part of your body that hurts
- **banging:** hitting hard
- **keeps:** continues to
- **splint:** metal stick you put on a broken arm, etc
- **surgery:** place where a doctor or vet works
- **turkey:** big bird
- **vet:** animal doctor

Two weeks later Dacty's wing is better. Helen and Roger want to see if he can fly. They wait until it is dark and they take Dacty outside into the garden in a big basket.
"Come on Dacty, now you can really fly," says Helen. But Dacty doesn't want to get out of the basket. He is holding his blanket• in his beak.
"I think he's cold," says Roger.
"I don't think so," says Helen. "He's afraid."
Helen and Roger take Dacty out of the basket. Roger climbs a tree.
"Come on, Dacty," he shouts. But Dacty quickly climbs back into the basket taking his blanket with him. "Let's take him back into the house and phone Aunt Elizabeth. She came back yesterday," Helen says.

Glossary

- **blanket:** thick warm cover

The Surprise

The children phone Aunt Elizabeth. They tell her that Dacty can't fly in Helen's room and he doesn't want to fly in the garden. Aunt Elizabeth tells them that pterodactyls lived at a time when it was very warm. "There were jungles• everywhere. Even in Greenland. So I think he likes warm temperatures," she says.

"But he can't fly in the house. He's too big now and mum hates him flying around," says Roger. "We need to find somewhere else• to keep him."

"Don't worry. I'll think of something," answers Aunt Elizabeth. An hour later she phones Roger and Helen. "I've got an idea," she says. "Get Dacty ready. I'll pick you up• in half an hour."

FLY TO ME, DACTY...

- **pick you up:** collect/get you with a car
- **jungles:** forests in a hot tropical country
- **somewhere else:** another place

Half an hour later Aunt Elizabeth arrives in her car. The children take Dacty and sit in the back of the car with him.

"Where are we going, Aunt Elizabeth?" they ask.

"To the museum. My office is very big. It's perfect for Dacty during the day. And at night, when the museum is empty, Dacty can fly around and look at all the wonderful things we have. I can't believe I didn't think of it before!"

"What will he eat?" asks Helen.

"There's a restaurant in the museum. The cook•, Mrs Robinson, is my friend. I can ask her to feed• Dacty."

Glossary

- **cook:** (here) person who cooks
- **feed:** give food to

The Surprise

At the museum they take Dacty out of the basket. He stretches● his wings and hops● on top of a stone lion.
"Can he see in the dark?" asks Roger.
"Yes, they see very well in the dark, just like owls●", explains Aunt Elizabeth.
"Look," shouts Helen. Dacty takes off● and flies high up. Then he lands on a stone statue. Aunt Elizabeth takes some sandwiches out of her bag. She holds them out● to Dacty. The pterodactyl flies down and takes them. Then he flies up to the top of the statue again.
"He likes it here," says Helen.
"Bye, Dacty," they shout.
"See you tomorrow."

- **holds them out:** offers them
- **hops:** jumps
- **owls:** night birds
- **stretches:** opens as much as he can
- **takes off:** starts flying

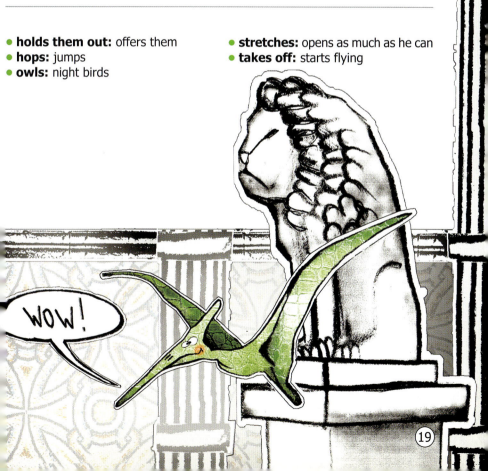

The Surprise

Six months pass and Dacty is very big now. During the day he sleeps in Aunt Elizabeth's office and at night he flies around the museum. But one night something strange happens. At midnight Dacty sees lights moving inside the museum. He flies closer to see what is happening. There are two men with torches• inside the museum. They are wearing masks and they are trying to open a case. Inside the case there is a mummy•.

Suddenly one man looks up and sees the pterodactyl. He is very scared. "Look, Bert," he says to the other man. "There is a huge• bird up there." The other man looks up, but Dacty doesn't move. "Shut up, Eric. Don't be silly. It's only a statue," the man says. "Come on. I'll open the case. You look for the gold medallions•."

While Bert tries to open the case, Dacty flies down and grabs Eric. The thief• is so scared that he can't say a thing. Dacty flies up and leaves him on top of a statue. He's stuck•.

Bert is so busy opening the case that he doesn't see what is happening. "Hey, where's the drill•?" he says, but there is no answer.

'Eric? Where are you, Eric?" he asks.

Then he looks up and sees his friend high above on the statue. Just then Dacty flies down again and grabs the second thief. He lifts him in his beak and carries him up to the statue. The two men are very afraid. They start shouting, but there is nobody there to hear them.

Glossary

• **drill:** thing you use to make holes
• **huge:** very big
• **medallions:** big medals
• **mummy:** very old body, wrapped in white bandages, usually of Egyptian kings or queens
• **stuck:** cannot move
• **thief:** person who takes/steals something that isn't theirs
• **torches:** small lights you can hold

In the morning when Aunt Elizabeth comes into the museum she hears the men shouting. Then she sees the broken mummy case.
"Help! Help! There's a monster in here," the men shout while Dacty flies down to her.
"First things first•," Aunt Elizabeth says. She goes into the restaurant, opens the door of the fridge and takes out some fish.
"Here you are, Dacty," she says and pets• his head. "Here's your breakfast. Thank you very much, you did a great job." Then she phones the police.

Glossary

- **first things first:** you say this when you want to do the most important things first
- **pets:** touches an animal gently

The mayor● shakes Dacty's wing and puts a big shiny medal over his head. "Congratulations, you did a great job."
Then he turns to Aunt Elizabeth, "What a great idea to have a big bird as a guard."
"Dacty's not a bird," Roger says, "He's a pterodactyl."
"Roger!" says Helen. "Don't say anything!"
"It doesn't matter●, children," says Aunt Elizabeth. "Dacty is a hero now." "A pterodactyl?" shouts another man.
"Wow! They love warm weather and jungles. I work in the Botanical Gardens●. We have a wonderful Palm House●. It's big and warm and just like a jungle. Your pterodactyl will love it there. We can feed him well and you can come to visit when you want."

- **Botanical Gardens:** place with lots of plants
- **it doesn't matter:** it's not important
- **mayor:** person who is boss in a town or city
- **Palm House:** glass house in Botanical Gardens with lots of tropical plants

The Surprise

So now Dacty is living in the Palm House at the Botanical Gardens. Roger and Helen visit him every day after school and bring him nice things to eat.
One evening Aunt Elizabeth comes with them.
"I'm going to Greenland again," she says. "I want to look for another egg in the ice. If I find the right egg maybe we can find a girlfriend for Dacty."
"And then we can have some baby Dacties, too!" shout the children.
"Can we come, too?" they ask.
Aunt Elizabeth smiles but she shakes her head●.
"Okay, Aunt Elizabeth," say the children. "Don't worry, Dacty. We'll stay with you!"

Glossary

● **shakes her head:** moves it from side to side to say 'no'

After Reading

1 Talk about Dacty. Ask and answer questions about Dacty using the words below.

> Has Dacty got any feathers?

> No, he hasn't.

feathers	beak	wing	bandage	fly	museum
warm weather	see in the dark	jungle	sausages	cold weather	

2 Now fill in the fact file about Dacty.

Type of Animal:.............................

Description:...................................

....

....

....

Food:...

Likes:..

Dislikes:..

Abilities:.......................................

3 Write a fact file for your pet or an animal you like.

After Reading

4 **In the story, Helen and Roger have a pterodactyl. In real life, people have some very strange pets too! Before reading the text about exotic pets, answer the questions below in pairs**

a) Can you name five exotic pets? **c)** How big do they grow?
b) Where do they come from? **d)** Are they dangerous?

5 **Read the text about exotic pets. Choose adjectives from the box below to complete the text.**

small	big	furry	trendy	nasty	wrong	long	~~popular~~

EXOTIC PETS

Nowadays, it is very (❌) *popular* to have a pet tarantula, a snake, a lizard or even a crocodile. Sadly, many of these pets die horrible deaths because their owners cannot look after them properly. They keep them in **(b)** .... spaces and they feed them the **(c)** .... food. But it's not only the pets that suffer! Many of their owners get **(d)** .... bites and have to go to hospital!
Reptiles can live for a **(e)** .... time in the wild and they can grow very **(f)** .... Monitor lizards grow to more than 1.8 metres and they can eat large animals, like the family dog or cat. Yes, before you run down to the pet shop to buy your **(g)** .... new pet, find out what it eats! You may need to feed your exotic pet with mice or locusts. How do you feel about that?
So before you buy that cute-looking lizard or that **(h)** .... spider, think very carefully.

6 **Now listen and check your answers.**

27

After Reading

1 Read Helen's email to a friend and choose the correct word for each space.

New Message

To:

Object:

Hi Anna,

You'll never guess what! You know my aunt Elizabeth likes travelling? This time she **(a)** .... to Greenland and she found a huge **(b)** .... in an ice cave there. She brought it back to England and she gave it to us. We put the egg in a cardboard box **(c)** .... the radiator. A few days later a bird came out of the egg. But it's not an ordinary bird. It's a pterodactyl!! He's very sweet. We call him Dacty. There's a problem! He gets **(d)** .... every day. Now he is too big for the house. Mum **(e)** .... him flying around and yesterday, he **(f)** .... his wing. He banged it on **(g)** .... furniture. He doesn't want to go outside. It's too **(h)** ....

Come and see him sometime.
Love Helen

(a)	**1** go	**2** went	**3** goes
(b)	**1** dinosaur	**2** sausage	**3** egg
(c)	**1** on	**2** next to	**3** in
(d)	**1** bigger	**2** the biggest	**3** big
(e)	**1** likes	**2** doesn't like	**3** liked
(f)	**1** hurt	**2** broke	**3** hurts
(g)	**1** a	**2** an	**3** the
(h)	**1** cold	**2** hot	**3** far

After Reading

2 Look at the pictures. Write what is happening.

a)

_____
_____

b)

_____
_____

c)

_____
_____

d)

_____
_____

3 Complete the summary of the story. Use the past simple of the verbs in the box.

be (x2)   take   stop   fly   enter   give   try   come   call   hurt   find

a) Aunt Elizabeth .... an egg in an ice cave in Greenland and she .... it to Helen and Roger to look after.

b) Inside the egg, there .... a baby pterodactyl. They .... it Dacty.

c) Dacty .... around the house and he .... his wing.

d) Aunt Elizabeth .... home and she .... Dacty to the museum.

e) One night some thieves .... the museum. They .... to steal some gold medallions but Dacty .... them. Dacty .... a hero.

29

After Reading

1 **Aunt Elizabeth is an explorer. Her hero is another famous explorer. Read the text about him and find the answers to the questions below.**

   a) Which pet travelled with him to the North and South Poles?
   b) What did he pull across the continent of Antarctica?

Sir Ranulph Fiennes - The Greatest Living Explorer

Sir Ranulph Fiennes is an English explorer and author and he holds many world exploration records.

1979 – 1982
Sir Ranulph Fiennes and Charles Burton were the first men to reach both the North and South Poles. Fiennes' Jack Russell dog called Bothie went with them. The expedition began in 1979 and ended on August 29th, 1982.

1992
In 1992, Fiennes and his team found the legendary Lost City of Ubar in the Rub al Khali desert of Oman near Ash Shisr. This ancient city disappeared around A.D. 300.

1993
In 1993, Fiennes and Dr Mike Stroud made the first walk across the continent of Antarctica without help. Each man pulled a 225-kilogramme sledge. This ninety-seven day trip was the longest polar journey in history.

After Reading

2 Why are these numbers important? Read the text and write a sentence about each one.
a) 300..
b) 225..
c) 97..

3 Find out about a famous explorer from your country. Write a short paragraph about him/her.

4 Explorers recently discovered the fossil of a huge dinosaur bone in Europe. Guess and circle the correct answers below. Then listen and check your answers.

a) Where did they discover it?
1 Italy   **2** England   **3** Spain

b) Which dinosaur was the bone from?
1 Pterodactyl   **2** Tyrannosaurus Rex   **3** Turiasaurus

c) Which part of the body did they find?
1 Its leg   **2** Its head   **3** Its tail

5 Listen again and tick T (true) or F (false).

	T	F
a) The dinosaur ate plants.	☐	☐
b) The dinosaur weighed 30 to 37 tonnes.	☐	☐
c) The dinosaur is 50 million years old.	☐	☐
d) The dinosaur bone was as big as a man.	☐	☐
e) One of its claws is as big as a leg.	☐	☐

After Reading

CROSSWORD

1 Read the clues and complete the crossword puzzle with words from the story.

a) The children put the egg in a cardboard box next to the ....
b) Dacty eats a lot of .... in the story.
c) When Aunt Elizabeth comes back from Greenland, she has got a .... for Helen and Roger.
d) "Dacty is a ....," Roger tells the vet.
e) The egg was in an .... cave in Greenland.
f) Dacty climbs into the basket with his warm ....
g) Aunt Elizabeth takes Dacty to live in the ....
h) Mum thinks that Dacty's name .... him.

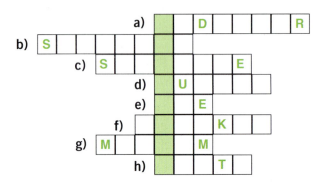

2 There is a mystery word in the puzzle. Complete the sentence below with the mystery word.

Pterodactyls are not birds. They are flying ....